THE INN AT THE FOREST'S EDGE

A FANTASY NOVELETTE

RAYMOND KEITH

The Inn at the Forest's Edge

Raymond Keith

https://authorraymondkeith.com

Copyright © 2023 Raymond Keith

ISBN eBook: 979-8-9892608-1-2

ISBN paperback: 979-8-9892608-0-5

Cover design: GetCovers.com

Author photo: EAH Creative

❀ Formatted with Vellum

To my enchanting bride,
Judy Rae,
who has supported so many of my "business" ideas, including
becoming an author. Thank you for always being by my side
through hard times and good.

ACKNOWLEDGMENTS

First and foremost, I thank the LORD, the Creator of all things and Master Storyteller, with whom we share His creative expression. He has given us His Word, the Lord Jesus Christ, who found me and saved me when I wasn't even looking for Him, yet needed Him desperately.

I would also like to thank:

My wife, Judy Rae, who loves books, but does not like fantasy. Thank you for reading many pages of my works and the vital feedback and encouragement you have given.

My beloved brother, John, who despite his busy life, always takes the time to read my drafts and give me his feedback and share in his creativity. You are a better writer than I ever will be. And also to his wife, Kathy, who also always encourages me and for your insightful advice.

Nora Lee Taylor, my friend and fellow author, who encouraged me to write down and share "the stories that God has given me" and introduced me to her editor.

Annette Bonner, editor, who published my first short story and always encouraged me to be a better writer.

Kimberly Lord, my friend and wise counselor, who also helped as a beta reader with encouraging feedback. Plus, you share my love of *The Lord of the Rings*.

To all my family, who always loves and supports me.

The great talents at GetCovers.com

All those at Realm Makers, who encourage us all to be better in every way for the Glory of God.

You, my readers, who have taken the time to read and hopefully enjoy this story.

CONTENTS

CHAPTER I

THE OFFER

J ohann guided his cart off the King's highway onto the dusty road. The mare plodded along in front of him, the only horse the meager family owned. The road was rough, but they knew every rock and rut, delivering milk, eggs, and cheese to their regular customers in exchange for other various goods, as well as coin. Their only customers were nearby neighbors and one small inn. The morning sun rose higher, and he had only one stop left—the inn. The small building sat far from its nearest neighbor, for few were so brave—or so foolish — to live on the edge of the wild. A vast forest stretched beyond and many mysterious tales were told about it. The forest changed the fates of men, both for their glory and, more often, for their destruction.

The road soon turned from dirt to a grassy two-track and the plowed fields fell away to grasslands with scattered trees. Johann enjoyed going to the inn, for they always treated him well. The owner was an older gentleman, short and lithe, which seemed unusual for an innkeeper. His sister was just as lean and slightly shorter, but they were both kind. The tavern's official name was "The Royal Stag" as the sign in front stated, but no one would have recognized that name. Everyone for many miles around only knew it as "The Inn at the Forest's Edge."

The place was a curiosity and had many stories of its own. Locals claimed of it being built generations ago by a crew of odd bearded men from unknown origins. Each block in the wall was hand cut, but no one knew where they got the white stone. Several unknown, large white barked trees with massive twisted trunks stood guard over the elegant structure. It seemed an odd location for an inn, but wayfarers stopped there occasionally, a few just out of curiosity. The lodging went unnoticed on the avoided forest road, for most preferred the longer King's Highway.

Just before the inn came into sight, a large white stag leaped onto the road in front of Johann. Deer often roamed the grassy fields along the forest's edge, but the youth had never seen one like this before, one so magnificent. Its sapphire eyes stared until they locked on his, drawing him into a vastness unfathomed, stirring in him a desire for something more. Something adventurous and exciting. Extraordinary or even supernatural. A longing for truths yet unknown. Time disappeared, and he knew not how long he stayed. The broad antlered creature leaped and continued on its way, soon lost in the chin-high grasses. The moment passed, but the longing settled deep into his soul, never to leave. His cart horse neighed, as if she too had understood the beauty of the event. When Johann reached his last stop, he pushed the incident out of his mind. He guided the cart up by the side kitchen door.

The mare tried to pull forward, for the innkeepers always gave her a treat by the stables.

"Whoa, Angel. You know the routine: unload first."

She looked back, saw that Johann was not agreeable, then

settled down to wait. He hopped down and reached for the door handle. As he did, the door opened and a young maiden stood staring at him face to face. He had never seen her before. He noticed immediately she was not at all like the other girls in town. The maiden had a radiance and maturity about her that was evident at a glance. At this moment, he understood why the last creature the Creator brought into being was the woman—for the woman was the most beautiful of all. She brushed a strand of honey glazed hair from her face. The rest flowed down her back from under the yellow headscarf that matched the ones worn by the innkeepers. Her eyes were the most engaging green. Not the green of olives that some have, but bright green like the new bud of a spring leaf or the first blades of grass in the morning sun.

After a moment of silence, it embarrassed him for staring. "You have green eyes," he blurted, still enchanted.

She gave a smile that lit up her countenance, revealing pearly white teeth. "Yes, so do you."

"I do? I ... I thought my eyes were blue."

"Well, they look green right now." She giggled. "My name is Faeyn."

His brimmed sun hat popped into his mind, and he snatched it off his head. "I am Johann."

"Nice to meet you." She brushed back the strand again. "I am staying with my uncle to help at the inn this summer."

"Really? Wow! I mean, nice to meet you, too."

Just then, the innkeeper came to the door. "I see you have met Faeyn. You better bring the milk in before it curdles. Then I want to speak to you."

"Yes, sir," Johann responded, and promptly unloaded. He was glad to do something, for he did not know what to say next. Faeyn spoke with Angel, kissed her on the nose and scratched her chin before going to the stable. When he had finished unloading, he went to find the innkeeper. His name was Erdan Silverfrond, and he reclined in the dining area.

"Please sit, Johann." The man gestured to a chair. "Morgrim, our stable hand, had some family matters come up, and he has to leave us for the summer. With your father's permission, would you be available to come work for us?"

"I would enjoy that, sir. What would I be doing exactly?"

"Taking care of the stables, of course, which also includes caring for the horses of any patrons of the inn. You would also help inside the inn as needed. Such as serving customers, assisting Miss Silverfrond in the kitchen, helping with the rooms, and doing repairs that come up. Assisting wherever needed. You may also need to taste test all the fresh baked honey cakes. Do you think you can do that?" His eyes lit up. Everyone loved her honey cakes. They were magical.

"I will do my best!"

"Are you sure you are not afraid to be living so near the forest for the summer?"

"Maybe, but I still want to do it, sir."

"Very well," stated Mr. Silverfrond, "When you get home, speak with your parents, and if agreeable, you can start next week when your family delivers the milk."

"I will speak with them as soon as I get home!"

Angel got her treat, and Johann was on his way, his heart filled with joy. This summer would surpass the dull routine of other years. Johann whistled as they trotted home. Angel picked up on the excitement coming from the boy and stepped up her pace. They would return home earlier than normal this week.

CHAPTER 2
SILVIAN

Johann's parents agreed, so his dad came along with him to do the deliveries and bring the wagon back home. Leery of the place, his dad asked questions until satisfied. The proprietors bought lots of goods and paid generously, making quality neighbors. They prearranged for his mother's sake that Johann would come home to get the milk and other goods for the inn once a week. They could use the inn's horses and wagons for the trip.

"Be a good lad. Work hard, do what you are told, stay out of trouble," his dad advised. "Make the family proud. Your mother and I taught you well. You know our ethics. I don't want to hear about any problems." Then he smiled. "I know you will do good. We already are proud of you. We'll miss you." He paused and his eyes grew serious once again. "One more thing. Stay out of the forest. It is a dangerous place. It is not the same as exploring the woods around the farm. Who knows what dangerous creatures live there?" His faced softened to his usual gentle expression. "We'll see you in a week and you can tell us all about your adventures!" His dad gave Johann a fatherly pat on the shoulder. With that, he loaded up and left after a last wave.

"You'll have to use Morgrim's room while he is gone. We need you out here in the stables," Mr. Silverfrond said.

"I get this whole room to myself?"

"It's small, but not too hot in the summer."

"No brothers to compete with, at least." The room attached to the barn smelled of pipe tobacco, sweat, and horses. Johann tried the bed. His feet hung over the end. He remembered Morgrim only reached his chest, even if his shoulders were twice the width. Still, the lad was pleased, and he made it a comfortable place.

After dropping his things in the room, Erdan took him to the stables. "It's up to you to keep the stables clean and to care for the animals. That's your primary job. We are...ahh...behind a bit, with Morgrim gone. It will take some work to get it proper again."

Johann looked the place over. There was plenty to do. "I'll get it clean." Johann stated. Erdan smiled at that response.

"There are three creatures to care for all the time. But you will also need to take care of any animals travelers bring with them, too." Johann nodded. "See that gelded Frisian over there? His name is Regal. You can use him to pull the wagon and go to your farm. Over there, the quarter horse. Her name is Nimble. We use her for riding sometimes."

"What about that one? I have seen nothing like him!" Johann pointed to a large, older stallion.

"That's Silvian. He came with Faeyn. He survived a great battle years ago. Treat him well."

Mr. Silverfrond showed him the tools and went back to the inn. One thing the locals respected was hard work, and Johann's family expected it, too. The new stable boy set to his task, determined to earn the Silverfrond's respect. Maybe Faeyn would notice.

After the innkeeper left, Silvian wandered into the stables. The creature watched the youth with a critical eye. He inspected every corner to be sure Johann did it right.

"Well, are you satisfied?" asked Johann with hands on his hips and a frown on his face. Silvian nodded his approval. Intelligence came through the eyes, and it seemed to understand everything he said. He didn't know how he knew, but he did. "How about a rubdown?"

Johann grabbed the brush and looked him over. The silvery beast saddened Johann. An old ugly scar marred his forehead. A few others dominated his chest, side, and rump. The scar on his right side was just behind the front leg and looked as if it had been a deep puncture, like a spear thrust. No fur grew around the wound. It was a shame, for Silvian must have been a real beauty in his youth. His coat had a white sheen, and his silky mane gleamed like no other that Johann had ever seen. A small beard accented his chin and feathering decorated his lower legs. His hoofs looked odd to Johann, almost like a goat's. He imagined a gallant knight or a mighty noble had owned him before.

The following week, Johann prepared the wagon for his weekly visit home. Johann grabbed a halter and headed out for Regal. But Silvian chased Regal away before approaching the youth.

"What are you up to? Mr. Silverfrond told me to use Regal." Johann went after Regal again, but Silvian got between them, nipping at the large Frisian who trotted off.

Johann glared at him. "Stop that! I got to get the milk! What do you want? More grain? A treat?" The equine shook his neck, poked at the halter, and stomped the ground. Silvian peered over at Faeyn hanging laundry, then back at the wagon.

He neighed at Johann. Faeyn glanced over, but continued her work.

"You want me to take you, instead?" Johann paced back and forth, uncertain. "Uh, I guess no one will mind."

Johann's family loved Silvian, and so did Angel, who started neighing when they were still down the lane. Silvian pulled the wagon expertly and seemed to know just where to go and what to do. No one complained, so Johann took him every week after that.

CHAPTER 3
BARALAS AND FAEYN

"After you finished cutting the wood, help Enna clean the large kettle," Mr. Silverfrond called. "Then check with Faeyn to be sure the rooms are ready." Johann beamed at the thought. He always delighted in spending time with her.

He also enjoyed just being at the inn, seeing the interesting people that would come by, and especially being near the woods. He spent his free time exploring the fields around the place and walking along the edge of the forest. Sometimes he would see animals, like squirrels and rabbits, songbirds and deer. He knew where each of them lived in just a few weeks. A large hawk always sat in the tree next to the inn and stables. He would talk to it every day, convinced that it was watching him all the time. The hawk acted most interested in the rodents and the doves, which it kept from getting into the grain. Johann named it the Gray Mouser. Faeyn giggled when she heard Johann talking to the accipiter. "His name is 'Medwin'," Faeyn corrected, "which means 'Sharp-eye'." But he continued to call it Gray Mouser.

"Don't wander too far into the woods, boy," a voice called to him one day. It was Baralas, the minstrel. "The forest is not as safe of a place as it seems here at the inn."

The minstrel reclined under a shade tree, tuning his lyre. Baralas seemed too grim for a minstrel, even though he pretended to be jovial in front of an audience. All of his outfits were of olive and black. His brimmed hat tied under his chin with flaps covering his ears. A red and yellow feather was the only bright color he allowed. Straight jet black hair reached down to his shoulder blades. It seemed he could not grow a beard—not a whisker. Not only did he play the lyre, but also the lute and a flute. Most of all, he was a master duelist and knife thrower. He set up several targets around the dining room and could stick a dagger in them from anywhere, slicing ribbons and snuffing candles as they spun. He even tossed his rapier with a thud and a twang that seemed to last forever. Every week, he put out a jar with a ten gold piece coin in it called a "pinnacle". Everyone prized the pinnacle except the very wealthy. A simple laborer like Johann needed to work over half a year to match its worth.

"Score on me thrice, and you win all that is in the jar," Baralas challenged. It cost a challenger five copper commons or a half silver coin called a 'daily,' which was considered a day's wages. Every coin gambled went into the jar, but he never lost. Few gave him even a challenge, despite their bravado of adventures or some training by such-and-such master. Baralas impressed Johann, but he didn't know what the minstrel thought of him. It surprised him that the man noticed him now, much less spoke to him. The bard would disappear sometimes, but always returned to stay at the inn, where the Silverfronds gave him a room for free.

Faeyn, on the other hand, was a carefree young maid who continually sang and laughed. She danced and swayed as she worked, as if she heard music he did not. She worked hard cleaning the rooms, assisting in the kitchen and helped to serve guests if needed. But the owners didn't like her interacting with the public too much.

"Too many uncouth men," Enna stated.

Faeyn, however, savored in meeting people and would talk with many of the guests. She loved their tales, even the ones that were obviously exaggerated or outright lies. She treated them all as absolute fact and listened with complete fascination. Faeyn would chatter with Johann, too, and listen to his stories about his family and living on the farm.

"I don't know why you want to hear about me and my family," Johann said. "It's not that exciting. Just taking care of the animals every day, planting, doing the chores, whatever. Boring really. It is more interesting here."

"Why do you think it is boring? I don't think so! Sounds like you have a wonderful family and life! Being on the farm, taking care of those precious animals. Your parents and siblings sound so sweet and nice! You should be thankful for those precious things! Many do not have that. It must be a wonderful place to grow up! Sounds so beautiful!"

"Yes, I guess it is. I enjoy working outside with the animals, seeing nature."

"Can I go with you tomorrow?"

"Huh? Go with me?" He paced back and forth, even as his heart soared at the idea of spending all day with her.

"Why not? I want to see it! Your farm!"

"Umm, I guess, if your uncle says it is okay."

"Really? Let's ask him right now!" Johann frowned, but followed her.

Her aunt and uncle sounded less excited by the idea and exchanged glances. "Well, I am not sure that is a good idea." Her uncle advised.

"Can you tell me why? What did my daddy say to you?"

"He said to watch over you and keep you safe. The country is quiet around here, true, but you never know who is on the road, especially near the Forest."

"Johann goes back and forth every week without trouble, don't you, Johann?"

Johann was trying not to be noticed, but now everyone looked at him. "Well, uh...yes, I never have any trouble. Except that one time, there was a rough-looking man..." The youth stopped when Faeyn glared at him. "But he didn't bother me at all," he muttered.

"Everyone knows Johann around here. He is a local young man," the aunt stated. Just then, Johann noticed Baralas listening in. The bard gave a quick nod to the Silverfronds, though Faeyn did not see. "Of course, I guess you won't be happy until you go see it. Let her go, Erdan."

"Very well, Enna. You can go, Faeyn. Johann, make sure you take Silvian. But only this once! And be back before dark!"

"Thank you!" She gave each a quick hug and left very pleased.

"Watch over that girl, boy," Erdan Silverfrond commanded. "Just to the farm and right back. No detours. Don't be too long, back before dark. Keep her safe. Understand?"

"Yes, sir!"

Mr. Silverfrond softened. "I trust you to act wisely. You have been doing a great job, young man."

CHAPTER 4
KEEP PRACTICING

The next morning, they set out. It was a beautiful sunny day and Johann regaled in the trip, listening to Faeyn chat away and delight in every flower, tree, and bird they saw. She was just as pleased at meeting Johann's family, and they were most charmed by her. Silvian seemed to have fun, too. They enjoyed a lunch with the whole family and then he showed her around the farm. He saw a hawk in a tree regarding them and he swore it looked just like Gray Mouser. Watched him the same way, too.

Johann wanted plenty of time to get back before dark, so they got the milk, eggs, and cheese and left in the early afternoon. As they turned out of the farm's lane onto the King's Highway, Johann saw a small man on a large, dark horse pop out onto the road from the fields. It was in the far distance, but right in the direction they were going. The man swung about and disappeared. Unease struck Johann, and he glanced at Faeyn. She did not seem to notice and was singing quietly to the bees and butterflies that were about. The horseman had acted strange, as if he did not want to be seen.

"A highwayman," Johann muttered to himself. Thieves were rare on this road as soldiers routinely patrolled, but robberies happened once in a while, and most often near the Forest's edge. Merchants regularly traveled the King's Highway, drawing unsavory men to this part of the kingdom. "The Silverfronds are counting on me," he thought to himself as he glanced at the beauty next to him.

Johann escalated the pace, and Silvian noticed his anxiety. They both remained alert as they passed the spot where Johann thought the man had been, but perceived nothing.

"Something wrong?" Faeyn asked. "Don't let my aunt and uncle worry you. Silvian won't let anything happen."

She sat up straighter and was now attentive to her surroundings, however. Johann kept looking in every direction as they went, wishing he had his hunting bow or a staff, or something he could use as a weapon. When they turned off the highway and got on the two-track, the trees increased, making him more nervous. Silvian gave a comforting neigh, and he relaxed a little. Finally, the inn came into view and he sighed.

Faeyn ran inside to exclaim all her adventures to her aunt and uncle as Johann put the wagon away.

"Where's Regal?" Johann pondered out loud as he was rubbing down Silvian. He repeated the question to Erdan when he found him.

"Baralas borrowed it...for an errand. He'll be back by dark."

Right at dusk, he brought the Friesian to Johann. Johann got up his nerve and spoke to Baralas. "Sir, can I ask something of you?"

"What is it?"

"Teach me to throw daggers." He blurted. "And maybe how to use a sword, too."

Baralas grimaced at him. "These are not toys, farm boy."

Johann's eyes drooped before recovering. "I understand. But I am not looking to walk around with one, just want to know how to use it. Today, I took Faeyn with me to my farm and family. There was a horseman. I feared he was a robber. I had no way of protecting her or myself. Teach me to do that."

"Most who carry swords die by others better than they are — or luckier. Swords bring trouble. And I am not a teacher."

Johann paced. "Maybe. But those with swords can still kill those without. At least if I know something, we would have some chance."

Baralas studied him for a moment, then pulled out a dagger and handed it to him. "This is one of my better daggers. Well balanced for throwing, but also good in a fight. Keep it. I have plenty. Take good care of it in the same way you do the stables. Tomorrow, after chores, I will teach you. Now, do your job, boy, and take care of Regal." Baralas turned and walked to the inn. He paused. "Just so you know, Faeyn is not helpless." Then he went in.

Johann smiled to himself, pleased not only by the excitement of learning, but also by earning the respect of Baralas. He had the pleasure of being with Faeyn all day, and now he even got a compliment from the bard! What a great day! That was the most the man had ever said to him before. He rubbed down Regal and put him out with the others. The others seemed glad to see him, the white stallion foremost.

The next day, Baralas showed him how to throw the dagger and told him to practice as much as he could. "Don't let it interfere with your chores, or I will stop teaching you."

Faeyn walked up behind them. "What are you doing, Johann?"

"I asked Baralas to teach me how to throw a dagger and knife fighting. And maybe use a sword, too." He hoped it impressed her. It did not. She watched for a short while, but soon left to play with the horses.

"Keep practicing," Baralas stated.

CHAPTER 5

CAPTAIN CAELAN

The inn was empty much of the time, being off the primary routes, not to mention being too near the forest. Johann didn't know how they paid the bills, but Erdan and Enna never worried about it. The patrons who did come were unique. Sometimes Lord Baldice's soldiers who patrolled the King's Highway came and would stay a night. The younger ones tested Baralas' skill, but the regulars knew better. He would also see adventurers of all sorts. Some were individuals, but predominantly they came in small groups. Most were traveling the King's Highway and came here out of curiosity, but some dared to venture into the Forest. There were also some unique men that were regulars, too.

"Those men with the war bows and special cloak pins. They are Qoholet. Ranger sages." Faeyn whispered.

"Ranger sages? Ko-ho-let? I assumed they were hunters."

"Shhh. You could say that. Hunters of evil beasts. And hunters of wisdom. Rangers sages. They have a secret abbey somewhere in a hidden valley north of here. Inside the edge of the forest, so they are not part of the kingdom."

"If it's a secret, how do you know about it?"

"My daddy knows their leaders."

"You never told me where you are from." His eyes followed as she went back to serving without answering.

Many of these rangers wore swords, but they never challenged Baralas. Most walked to the inn from somewhere. Maybe Faeyn told him the truth. They said little, but treated him well. He showed these men more respect after that.

Johann also recognized some locals on the last days of the week. They came to enjoy the entertainment, see what characters were around, and take a break from their labors.

Almost all the patrons were men, but he also saw women of all sorts, too. From finely appareled merchants to independent female adventurers with weapons or spell books, to provocatively dressed prostitutes and "gold diggers." The Silverfronds did not let the working girls ply their trade at the inn, but usually they were accompanying men with money in their pockets, even if that was just temporary.

"You are a cutie! Why don't you sit here with us?" They would sometimes tease Johann. Women of every cultural class flirted, which shocked the youth. It did not seem to matter what their social status appeared to be. He always turned beet red, invoking chuckles from the patrons and scowls from Faeyn. Sometimes their provocative dress was enough to make him uncomfortable, which encouraged more flirtations and giggles. Some days, it was hard to guard his eyes, and some made it even harder.

One day, a horseman approached the inn in the early afternoon when the inn was quiet. Outfitted in mail, a shield and a helm hung from his saddle, and a long sword sat at his waist. He looked familiar with each of these items. Gray touched his dark beard and hair. A bedroll and saddle bags rested behind the saddle. He was not one of Lord Baldice's men or even one of the king's knights. A mercenary.

"I will not be staying the night, young man. So don't unsaddle him. And be careful, he's a trained warhorse. Where is the innkeeper?"

"Yes sir! Let me secure your stallion and I will take you to Mr. Silverfrond."

"Greetings, Mr. Silverfrond. I am Captain Caelan. A coalition of merchants hired me to get them safely to the eastern kingdoms—through the Forest."

Erdan nodded. "How many wagons? How many mouths? What supplies will they need from me?"

"The king states we must have a minimum of twenty wagons and forty fighting men. We travel at our own risk, but you know that decree, I am sure. The train counts twenty-one wagons, forty-five soldiers, forty-eight civilians, and sixty-five animals. We will equip ourselves with enough supplies, but intend to stop here for 2 nights—one full day—and restock what we consume during our journey here. Can you handle that?"

"When?"

"They are on their way already. They will be here in three days. Is that a problem?"

"No problem. We are well stocked. Just need a few more details to best serve you. I will also notify the bard to make your stay more pleasurable."

"Very good. Many will just sleep in the wagons or camp in the grass, and some soldiers can use the stables if there is room. I am sure some merchants will set up to ply their trade whilst here for the day. With your permission."

"Agreeable," Erdan stated. "We will pass the word to any locals of the opportunity." Erdan studied the man before adding, "Let me ask you, Captain. Have you or any others traveled the Forest Road before?"

"Yes, this will be my third. I traveled in each direction once. It is a minimum of twenty-five days from this inn to the gate on the other side. The first few and the last few days are not too bad, but for most travelers, the rest of the time is pure fear. They hired me and my men for that reason. Almost all of those in my unit have gone under the canopy at least once."

"Impressive. I wish you all the best on your journey."

CHAPTER 6
THE CARAVAN

As scheduled, late in the afternoon of the third day, Captain Caelan, astride his warhorse, led a large caravan up the grassy two-track. He stopped once again in front of the inn, and Johann was there to take his horse.

"Take good care of him. We have a long journey ahead of us," Caelan said. Johann nodded and led the stallion to the stables.

Caelan barked orders to the soldiers riding alongside the caravan and directing the wagons about. The wagons were of all sorts, from basic cloth covered wagons to colorful enclosed ones. Many set out their wares in hopes of a sale or two to anyone at the inn, but there were few customers. A few locals and even a ranger or two stopped by to look at the hand spun cloths, silk scarves, woolen blankets, cow hides, leather works, iron tools, wooden tools, jewelry, pottery, potions, books, scrolls, spices, and even a few weapons. The kingdom's resources were primarily agricultural (such as cattle, sheep, horses, and grains). A few daring merchants brought some quality livestock, hoping to get breeding fees. Other lesser stock appeared to be a traveling food source. Tents sprang up on the grass lawn on the east side of the inn and along the road. Some soldiers just slept on the ground as the weather was clear and warm. The wealthier stayed in rooms, as it was the last comfortable bed for almost a month.

The Silverfronds insisted Faeyn keep a low profile, cleaning rooms only. Johann kept very busy, however, helping the merchants and soldiers with their horses and livestock.

"Use care with my steed, stable boy," harassed one of the young mercenaries named Jesper. "Or I will mark you." He then drew his sword and lightly smacked Johann's arm with the flat of the blade. "That is just a taste." Thick dark hair covered Jesper's head, accented by a thin beard. Many young women liked his sharp almond eyes. Johann heard the youth brag of his martial training and took time to belittle Johann when he could. Johann ignored and avoided the man as he was able, but was determined not to let it change his routine or fail in his duties. He overheard Jesper bragging more than once. "Rumors exaggerate the forest's danger. Why, I accompanied Lord Baldice on a boar hunt once south of here. Except for the impressive boar we killed, I saw nothing to cause such fear. Just silly stories by the timid locals, I am convinced."

Johann didn't believe him. He was just one of the common soldiers and younger than most. He tried to flirt with Faeyn a few times. Faeyn gave Jesper the cold shoulder each time. Johann's jaw got sore from all the teeth clenching he did during the caravan's stay. He warned Jesper to be more respectful to her the second day, but the man just laughed at him. Drawing his sword again, Jesper smacked him until Johann was red all over. He realized that Baralas had spoken true about swords. If he had one now, he might have attacked Jesper, probably getting himself injured or even killed. At the very least, he would have received even more mockery from the bully. Johann continued practicing with Baralas, but knew he was not ready to duel. It made him more than ever determined to improve. He imagined putting a few throwing daggers into the man, but restrained himself.

"You never know, Johann. With a sword in hand, you may have avoided the beating. That is a possibility, too." He said to himself as he stomped about cleaning the stables.

After the sword whipping, Caelan stepped in and ordered Jesper to leave her and Johann alone, and everyone respected the captain or feared him. Jesper challenged Baralas that night and did well, to Johann's annoyance. But the minstrel tired of his tongue and quickly marked him thrice. The failed duel had no effect on the man's ego, unfortunately, claiming he did better than any of the other challengers.

Meanwhile, Silvian scrutinized all the soldier's horses and other animals about and seemed to visit with each one that he could reach. They all respected him and came under his authority, even the fiery warhorse of Caelan. To get Johann's attention, Silvian would kick at the gate with his front hooves.

"I know you want out, but I'm too busy!" Somehow, Silvian got out anyway. Johann never figured out how, assuming he jumped the fence. Despite their disagreement, Silvian made Johann's work easier by keeping all the animals in order during their stay.

All at the inn rejoiced to see them off on the second morning. Captain Caelan desired to leave at dawn, but it took until late morning to get them all moving. He paid Erdan well, thanked him for the hospitality and planned to return from the east leading a train next spring.

Jesper seemed glad to be going. "I don't know how anyone slept with all that noise and flashes of light. Oddest thing I ever experienced." Faeyn giggled when she heard that. No one else noticed anything. Jesper took one last chance to insult Johann before he rode off. Johann scowled but soon realized the bully was really a smaller man, even if Johann never matched his fighting skills. Jesper demonstrated a shallow and self-centered character. Johann preferred to emulate the knights of the realm who practiced kindness, selflessness, and morality.

CHAPTER 7
A DUEL, IF YOU PLEASE

After that, little happened at the inn until Mid-Summer's eve. Only one patron sat dining. He dressed himself in silks, so all assumed that he was a noble, or at least a merchant. His attire was all in bright colors, even gaudy, and the style seemed foreign. A thin, pointed nose dominated his narrow face. He kept his thin beard trimmed close, the red of his hair and beard both accented by white at the chin and ears. One thing that was odd, and there was a plethora of things that were odd about the fellow, was he did not have any servants or bodyguards. He had arrived alone and on foot. Johann could only see a fox whenever he looked at him, and he did not feel comfortable standing close to the man. The patron sat quietly, sipping the best wine in the house with a winsome grin on his face as he pawed through a scroll on the table, peering down through reading glasses. But the scroll seemed not to be his only interest. The corners of his dark eyes followed the staff about as they worked. He concentrated on Baralas, but noticed Faeyn as well. The only one he showed no interest in was Johann, who soon retired to his room.

As the evening wore on, Johann woke again. The low burned candles in the dining area windows showed it was not yet midnight. Getting out of bed, he peeked in through a window to get a last look at the stranger. A bowl and a plate sat on the table in front of him with just a few pieces of bread crusts. The wine glass was still there, but was less than half full. As the clock struck midnight, the nobleman stood up and finish his wine. He looked about to see that the innkeeper and Baralas were the only ones left not in bed.

In a growling, yet slippery voice, his winsome smile never leaving his face, he stated to Baralas, "Bard, a duel, if you please." Johann crept closer to hear and see better, even moving up to crack open the door and peek in.

"Very well," stated Baralas, a little leery of the man, but still confident.

"A pinnacle, yes?" asked the man, as if he had trouble with the common tongue.

"If you score thrice, yes," confirmed the minstrel.

The man bowed and chose one of the practice swords. It just dawned on Johann that the man had no visible weapons on his person, not even a dagger. With a few test slashes, he showed he was ready by taking a defensive stance. Baralas took the other dueling weapon and prepared himself. The patron tested the bard with a few thrusts and swipes, but nothing serious and the bard easily defended. Baralas usually let his opponents engage a few times before scoring the first mark, and so it went this time, with a clean touch on the stranger's forearm. The man acknowledged the score with a nod and a tab on his arm, before engaging again. But now a coldness touched his eyes, and he came like a whirlwind, managing an easy slice to Baralas's thigh. The minstrel bowed and stated, "one each." Baralas's eyes also changed, Johann noticed, and the duel increased in tension. The air tingled, setting Johann's hair on end. The two now engaged in the most realistic encounter Johann had yet to witness as the masters circled, feinting and thrusting, cutting and parrying. In the next instant, the patron feigned and thrust, arching the blade on the chest of the bard.

Baralas, again, bowed at the neck, "two to one, challenger's advantage," before preparing himself a third time.

"I know who you are," growled the man abruptly. "I know who you all are," as his grin broadened. "Except that stable boy, who looks like a local nobody." Then he attacked again, and Baralas did all he could to defend himself. To Johann's astonishment, the bard finally succumbed as his opponent pinned him to the wall. The mysterious man pressed the blunt point on the bard's chest, the winsome grin never leaving his face. "And I plan to sell that information. So be warned." Then he stepped back, bowed, and returned the sword to the wooden tube he had removed it from.

"The pinnacle," He stated with his hand out.

"One pinnacle, worth ten gold, as promised and earned," Baralas confirmed, and gave the coin to him. But the bard's eyes followed every move of the victor and his left hand gripped a dagger at his belt.

"A pleasure." He stepped over to his table. The man gathered up his scroll, book, and other items and headed for the door. Johann dodged back into the shadows and watched the man walk out into the night. He followed at a distance and noticed that the rich stranger did not head towards civilization, but took the lane right into the forest with a steady stride —alone. Johann followed as far as the edge of the trees, but then the darkness swallowed the man. Just before disappearing from view, Johann swore he saw a bushy canine's tail popping out from under his cloak as he dropped to all fours, but it could just have been the moonlight. Johann poked his head in the dining room to find Baralas and Erdan intensely whispering together. He laid down again, but did not sleep for a while.

CHAPTER 8
VOICES IN THE DARK

"Wake up! Johann! Wake up, young man!" Johann bolted his eyes open and sat up. "Hurry!"

The week following Mid-summer's eve had been uneventful at the inn. Baralas spent more time working with him on training with the dagger and sword after chores. He was decent at throwing, improving at knife fighting, but was still fairly basic at swordsmanship. The day before had been a hard one—hot, humid, and draining. Johann had been deep in sleep when the voice pierced his dreams.

"Come quickly! To the east yard! We need your help now!" As Johann forced himself awake, grabbed his clothes, and stumbled outside, he suddenly realized that the voice came not from the yard or the inn, but the words were being implanted into his head! "Yes, this is Silvian! This way! Come here now!" Johann became more alert, but just as confused as he came face to face with the creature. "Blessed, but you are hard to wake, even with someone screaming in your head. Follow me now!" The voice echoed in his skull as he ran after the white beast to the eastern side of the inn. As Johann stumbled behind, he contemplated if he was still dreaming. Somehow Silvian got out of the stables again. And was that blood on his face?

Out on the lawn, Johann could not be sure what he was seeing. It looked like bodies sprawled on the ground in the moonlight. "Johann! Thank Amilye, you are safe at least!" Johann followed the voice to the corner of the inn. A lantern on the ground lit the grieved face of Enna as she held Erdan in her arms next to the inn walls. "Will Baralas live?"

"Yes, save him," Erdan pleaded. "I will live. Enna helped me." Johann realized the innkeeper had his arm across his gut. He now looked down at the mound and saw that it was an unconscious Baralas, covered in blood from multiple wounds. At least, he hoped he was unconscious.

"He is going to survive. He's stable," Silvian invaded his confused thoughts. "That is all I can do for now. It will take time for him to recover, but he will recover. Time we do not have. Erdan, I have nothing left for you."

"We are fine. I healed the wound well enough for now," Enna replied. "But Faeyn! We need to save her! What can we do? They took her!"

The words crushed Johann, and he felt lost. He now noticed that the other smaller mounds were also bodies— bodies of small, ugly creatures the size of children. He counted eight of them and all were dead, laying in bloody heaps. Two sported blackened burn marks on their chests. Baralas's dagger was still in one of them. Johann pulled out the dagger and wiped the dark blood on the dead creature's tunic.

"Johann! You must go with Silvian!" a hand gripped his ankle. It was Baralas. "Go now. Take my weapons. Find Faeyn!" He had raised his head, but now laid down again and loosened his grip. Johann looked at him again and in the moonlight, saw his ears for the very first time. The tops curved up into elongated points.

"Quickly. I have failed," Baralas added in a whisper.

"Yes, that is best." Silvian agreed. "Johann, get your gear—daggers, bow, arrows, cloak—now. Enna, get some food for him. Erdan, you must notify the king! Johann and I will find her. Rest Baralas, Medwin has gone after them. We will find her. It is Krath. The warlock sent them, I am sure." Silvian took charge, Johann realized as he ran to get his things. A horse? In command? What horse ruled over men? What horse speaks into people's minds! Where did these creatures come from? And Baralas's ears! Was he even a man? I must still be dreaming! But he feared for Faeyn and did not hesitate or question anything yet, just did what he was told. But what could he possibly do as a simple sixteen-year-old farmer's son? He was just a stable boy!

Silvian waited outside his door when he came out. "On my back—now. We ride in haste. No time for saddles or reins. I will explain everything as we go." Johann slung his bow on his back, his quiver on his belt, and thrust the two daggers into his belt. One in front and one at his back. He had a small backpack and Enna ran out with some cheese, jerky, bread, and a skin of water. He pulled himself up on Silvian and they rushed off before he even got his legs all the way around his girth. Regal and Nimble both called out after them, wanting to follow. They galloped into the VenKeth, known as the Venerable Woods.

CHAPTER 9
UNICORNS AND ELFIN

"I know you have questions," Silvian spoke as they ran. "Faeyn's life is in danger. You must listen to everything I say, for her sake. Do you understand? It is up to me and you — maybe you more so---to help her. There is no one else. You will need to be brave, my friend. Muster your courage; overcome any fear." As the creature spoke, Johann felt a panic rising in himself, but he pressed it down before it paralyzed him. He felt so overwhelmed. A shiver ran through the boy, but then he calmed down.

"Listen to me closely. Everything at the inn is not what it appears. Much of what you may think of as myths have truth in them. There are genuine parts to many of the stories. Try to understand. I am not a horse, as you assumed. I am a unicorn. The Silverfronds, Baralas, and even Faeyn are not humans. They are what you would call elfin." Silvian paused in his speech to see if Johann comprehended. Johann said nothing, but tried to process what the talking beast was saying. Elfin? Unicorn? Johann considered all the strange things he had encountered in the past few months, and he realized that the creature's words held some truth, but part of him feared it was an elaborate ruse. The words and thoughts continued in his mind. "Baralas almost died. That is real goblin blood on that dagger. I am really talking to you with telepathy. This is not a ruse, though we deceived you about who we are, and for that, I am sorry. It was for a greater purpose of safety for us all."

Johann finally found his voice. "Don't unicorns have horns?"

"Yes, that is true. You have seen my scars. Scoundrels cut my horn off years ago. I once ruled a realm, like your king. It was a small woodland realm, but wondrous. Invaders came, and I almost died defending it. They left me for dead. They took my horn as spoils. Unicorn horns are extremely valuable in the black markets. Unicorns heal others with their horns, so evil creatures take them for magic potions and for other wicked purposes. I still have some power of healing, but the horn held much of my strength. That is why I barely saved Baralas. But most do not know that a unicorn's horn starts at the base of the skull, not the top. There is still a little left. The elfin rescued me and cared for me, so now I serve them. I owe them my life."

Johann nodded. He reasoned it may be true and believable. "Baralas had pointed ears, like the elfin stories. They all covered their heads to hide them."

"Many, many years ago, the elfin king, Faeyn's grandfather, wanted to learn more about men and observe them. So he built the inn with the help of the dwarfin. Morgrim, the former stable hand, is dwarfin. Your king knows all about these things. His ancestor approved it. The elfin lord commissioned Erdan and Enna with running the inn and sending information back. Faeyn is the present king's youngest daughter---yes, she is really an elfin princess----and she desired to learn firsthand about humans."

It all overwhelmed Johann. He has been gushing over an elfin princess?! Johann turned beet red, thinking of how foolish he must have acted sometimes. Thankfully, there was no one to see it in the dark of the deserted forest road. She probably thought of him as a boyish simpleton!

"Concentrate and watch for enemies! We are in danger and so is she! And do not worry, we all like you. Did we not all agree to have you come to work at the inn? Now, put yourself aside and pay attention to me! And watch the forest! Her father agreed she could work at the inn for the summer. It has always been a safe place. Baralas is more than a bard. He came as her personal bodyguard. Medwin the hawk and myself were all sent to protect her. Erden and Enna are capable magic-users. Morgrim is a sturdy foe. We would all give our lives for her. No one should have known she was even here. Faeyn herself knows some magic and has some training with weapons. Morgrim truly had family issues and left. But I am convinced it was that fiend who showed up on Mid-Summer's eve. He must have told Krath." He paused. Johann asked about Krath and the fiend when Silvian silenced him. "Quiet!"

Silvian halted with little warning. They now stood several miles from the inn on the forest road, but it seemed deep in the dark forest to Johann hours before dawn. The road had climbed steadily up to Threshold Pass at the top of the ridge, though Johann had never heard of the place. He looked about, every nerve on edge, with one hand on a dagger and the other gripping the unicorn's mane with vice-like intensity.

"Something happened ahead," Silvian whispered in his mind.

CHAPTER 10

DECISIONS

The unicorn shuffled forward for several dozen yards, then stopped again. "As stealthy as you can, hop down and look on the left side of the road by the bushes. Careful!"

Johann slid down and pulled out his bow and an arrow. Even in the moonlight, the trees made it impossible to see much. The hair on his neck was all standing up and his body shook, but he crept forward as quietly as possible. He stayed in the center of the road as long as he could, as he feared to get close to the road's edge.

"To the left, check the bushes. Be brave." Silvian encouraged.

Johann saw something dark on the road and bushes. Blood? His ears magnified every crunch of stone and the snap of a twig beneath his feet, every creak of a branch from the woods. The forest itself remained stone quiet. Finally, he moved off the road and into the bushes. Something was there. A large dark lump or mound. As he inched forward, he saw the goblins' faces and let out a gasp as he released his arrow.

Nothing moved. He crept closer after what seemed like several minutes and saw the goblins' bodies lying in a row. "They're dead," Johann stated out loud.

"Talk to me in your mind, don't yell," Silvian coached. "How many? Can you tell me anything?"

Johann concentrated inside his head. "Four. It looks like puncture wounds to me. Maybe arrows?"

"Very good! I can understand you! Any arrows still in them?"

"No. Someone stacked their weapons and gear next to them. Wait, here's a broken shaft, but no tip."

Silvian came closer. "The arrow appears to be of human design. Maybe we have an ally nearby. Rangers patrol the pass sometimes. That is good news, as this may have been an ambush set for us. Medwin followed the princess. Perhaps he knows what happened. We need to find him if not the princess. On my back! But we must be alert!"

"Wait! Let me take a sword."

"It may be wise. You have some training. Be quick."

Johann looked at the goblin weapons in the dark as best he could. The arrows were too short, and he had enough of his own. He found a short sword that fit his hand, though not perfectly, so he grabbed a belt and scabbard. The belt barely reached, but he made it work. He felt a little better equipped to meet enemies now.

The two of them continued on the road as it descended on the other side of the ridge, giving Johann the feeling of dropping into a dark pit. They were in the mystic part of the forest now. Silvian kept to a slower pace than before, his ears fixed forward, attuned to every sound as he probed ahead with his mind. There was no more talking of any kind. Johann moved past the initial shock of all that he just discovered, but the reality of the danger he was in multiplied. If it had only been about himself, he would have fled long ago, but whenever he felt ready to flee, he remembered Faeyn.

After several more miles, with dawn still a few hours away, Silvian slowed from a trot to a walk. They had come off the ridge and were now in the flats of the forested plain. The unicorn came to a stop but said nothing. Johann heard something in the bushes ahead. Silvian just stood like a statue and Johann feared to move. His bow was still in his left hand, but he was afraid to let go of the unicorn's mane and reach for an arrow. Either he would fall off or make too much noise. Silvian trotted forward several lengths than stopped. Johann whipped out a shaft as something hopped out of the bush. It was a bird with an arrow in its left wing. As it fluttered about, Johann recognized Gray Mouser. He slid down and gently moved towards the accipiter. The hawk calmed down and let him look at the wing. In the dark it was hard to see, but the arrow had only damaged feathers, not muscle. It was only hindering flight. As gently as he could, Johann pushed the shaft through the wing until it came out. The raptor whistled out a cheerful call.

"Medwin says thank you," Silvian relayed to him. "He also stated that his name is not Gray Mouser, but he appreciates the compliment. 'Sharp-Eye' in the common tongue, if you prefer." Did everyone—even this bird—know what was going on but Johann? "He states he lost the kidnappers and the princess, but they left the road here and headed south on a narrow trail. With the arrow free, he can make his way back to the King for help. He can not fly far at a time, only short flights, but he will not stop until he reaches help. We must do the same. We must watch for Krath and his goblins. They may be nearby."

Johann marked the place by sticking the goblin arrow in the ground and tying his kerchief on it as best he could. Moving off the road, Johann looked around until he found the hidden trail. From here on out, he would travel by foot through the trees, in front of the unicorn. He kept his bow in his hand, with an arrow notched. He reached down and touched the dagger multiple times as he stalked through the trees. It was slow going as they tried to be as quiet as possible, with constant stops to listen.

"I sense beings of corrupt nature ahead," Silvian placed in Johann's mind. "Goblins, to be sure."

He nodded back in his mind. He continued forward and saw the faint glow of a fire on large rocky outcroppings in the distance ahead.

"There." He stopped and took a deep breath. Fear crept back into his bones, but he pushed it aside.

"You must sneak up and see if the princess is there. If she is, you must help her. I cannot. You must do this. Be strong and courageous."

Johann knew this was true, but he feared failure. He feared it more than he did death. Failure specifically in the form of cowardice. The idea of potential torture did not sound appealing, either. Johann crept forward before he thought about it too much. He focused his concentration on being as quiet as possible. As he got closer, the glow increased. The reflection of the flames danced on the walls of the rocks. Faint whiffs of smoke and other foul odors caught his nose, such as the stench of men who had not bathed for weeks. He heard the occasional clang of movement, like metal on rock or the squeak of leather. A small band had camped amid a group of huge rocks jutting out of the ground. He moved to the right, off the trail, and hid in the bushes to peer between the rocks before he got too close. Now he could see a few of them. They were goblins for sure, not men. About three feet tall or maybe a little more. Scrawny, over-sized pointed ears, huge ugly noses and mostly or completely bald. All the ones he saw seemed to be sleeping, or at least resting. Their clothes seemed little more than rags or sewn skins, though most also wore leather breast armor. Small swords, javelins and bows laid close by. Johann continued moving closer, trying to remain hidden by the bushes and rocks. All he saw appeared to be asleep. He counted six goblins so far.

Finally, he came up to the rock and crawled up onto a lip, shielding his body from view but peeking over into the camp. He held the scabbard to keep it from scraping or clanging. He counted over six, more like nine or ten. At least twenty goblins attacked the inn, he guessed based on the dead ones at the inn and along the road, assuming this was the raiding party. Only two of them seemed to be awake, but they also lounged in a relaxed fashion, poking the fire and drinking fermented liquids. They both looked half asleep as well. Over in the corner of the camp lay Faeyn, curled up in a ball near the fire. She was not too close, as if they had just dumped her there.

Johann studied the situation, trying to figure out what to do. He was not used to making important decisions on his own. He had always followed his parents or his siblings or other adults. At the inn, he listened to the Silverfronds and Baralas. The youth always let everyone else decide, and he did his best to accomplish those decisions. He saw himself as a good and dedicated follower, appreciated by his superiors for his loyalty and hard work. He was a team player, not the captain. Even Silvian, who just a few hours ago he thought was just an unintelligent animal, Johann followed willingly. But now it was just him and he did not know what to do. He knew nothing about goblins or elfin or even princesses. He knew nothing about rescuing people or much about fighting, either. What could he possibly do? They outnumbered him and trained with better weapons.

But Johann knew he had to do something. He could not

leave Faeyn, someone he admired and cared about, a young woman they told him to protect, in the hands of wicked enemies without trying. So, without realizing it, he made a decision. A big decision. And in doing this, it would change him forever, though it would not fully ripen for several years. He decided to do something instead of doing nothing. He decided to be brave and try to help her and not run away, even if it failed. Even if it cost him his life. It was the right thing to do. In deciding, he started down a path of learning how to be a leader and bear the responsibility that came with it.

CHAPTER II
CREEPING AND CRAWLING

So now that he committed himself to a rescue, what could he do? What skills did he have? He was not unintelligent. And he was good at hunting and being stealthy. He had a bow and a quiver of arrows, a short sword, two daggers and some training with Baralas, thankfully. He stood taller than the goblins and he guessed stronger. But if they overcame Baralas, a skilled elfin, what could he do? Being creatures of the night, he guessed they had better night vision. Their ears and noses were big compared to their face. Maybe better hearing or smelling, too? There were too many to shoot with his arrows, assuming he could fire accurately without shaking. At most, he could injure or even kill one or two, then the rest would be on him. He could try to kill them in their sleep one at a time, but didn't think he could pull it off. He had never killed before, except a few birds and small game while hunting.

Finally, he decided on an idea. If he moved around the camp, he may reach her without the two noticing or waking the others and sneak her out of camp. If successful, Silvian could speed them away to safety. He took one last look for details, then slipped back down off the lip.

It seemed forever getting through the bushes to get to where he believed Faeyn was lying. He needed to be stealthy, so that meant quiet, which meant slow. Plus, he circled around wide to avoid any patrols noticing him, not that there seemed to be any. Dawn had to be soon, he estimated. He planned to use the predawn light to his advantage. Having a sword strapped to his hip was a new thing, and it got caught in the brush a few times until he figured out a system. When he reached near where he guessed the princess lay, he paused. All seemed quiet in the camp, though he thought he heard something moving in the distance to the southeast. Perhaps animals stirring with the coming dawn. If there were birds about, they did not make a sound.

Hearing nothing, he eased the sword out of its leather sheath and crept forward on his belly, wishing Baralas or even Silvian were with him to confirm he was doing the best thing. He left his bow and quiver in the bushes. As he got past the edge of the rocks looming about him, he could see that the fire burned down to little more than glowing embers. Crawling limited his vision of most of the camp, but all seemed to be still yet. No goblins stirred. Faeyn lay just a stone's throw away, facing the rock with her eyes closed. He could see now that they tied her to a pole at her hands and feet. They must have carried her on their shoulders like a hunted deer.

He studied the distance between him and her. Five paces exposed to the view of the drooping goblins by the glowing embers. Hands and sword in front, he scurried forward. The five paces seemed a mile. Using her body as a shield from view, he slipped between her and the rock wall. How beautiful she looked, even in the faint light. Even in her dirty nightgown with its small tears from the brush; even with her hair in a mess, her pointed ears exposed, and dirt on her face. He soaked in her beauty, from her dainty feet to her delicate hands to her honey hair and smooth skin. When he came face to face, she opened her eyes. A sad smile formed as tears ran down her cheek. He put his finger to his lips for silence and began slicing at the ropes. First her hands, then her feet as she held the pole to keep it from clanging. She read his mind! As he worked, he imagined making enough noise to match the banging of pots together in a kitchen, but none of the goblins rushed over. Once he freed her, he raised his head to look beyond her. No movement from the camp. He nodded, and they began the long crawl to the brush. He let her go first. The darkness faded away, but it was not yet light. Not too fast, stay quiet, he kept thinking to himself as he wanted to grab her hand, get up and start running. But he didn't. Elation crept over him as they pulled past the rock wall and into the bushes. He looked back once more into the camp. Nothing! He couldn't believe it!

She squeezed his hand as they raised on their hands and knees, creeping away from the rocks. He planned to grab his quiver and bow before leaving. Just then, a giant dark shadow stood up in front of them, a heavy spear in its hand. A scream escaped from Faeyn. Johann swallowed his. More tall figures stood behind the first.

CHAPTER 12
KRATH THE WARLOCK

"Leaving us so soon, Princess?" snarled the giant. Johann soon realized that he was a goblin, not a giant, with the same large, pointed ears and an over-sized nose. Just far larger than any of the rest he had seen. He was not as gigantic as he first imagined, but still big enough. Even with a hunched back, he matched the height of a tall man. The skin was a grayish-green. He had heavy forearms and shoulders and a strong back with just a small pudge at the belly. His arms were extra long and crisscrossed with scars, both old and new from his witchcraft and divination. Scars marked his thighs as well. Dark, greasy hair discolored his limbs, chest and back, more similar to a man than that of a beast. A few dozen dark hairs dotted his chin and jawline, and the same number was on his bald head. Branded into his arms were strange runes, and tattooed black dots decorated his dark eyes. His sneer seemed permanent, showing long yellowish teeth, the fangs slightly longer on both top and bottom. Long, pointed ears stuck out beyond his bald head, reaching up as high as the center ridge of his skull. The hands and bare feet had thick sharp nails jammed with dirt. The goblin king, for that is who he was, covered himself in a knee-length tunic of sewn wolf-hides open to the navel, revealing the armor underneath. A heavy hemp rope wrapped around his waist with a stained, unsheathed knife tucked behind it. His breast plate was of boiled leather studded with broken bones. His right hand held a heavy spear. The left gripped the center boss of a round iron-banded shield. A human slave stood next to him carrying an over-sized menacing iron mace. Behind him, Johann could now see more goblins, lots more. Those closest to the leader equaled the size of large men and looked military. Boars. The rest of the troops seemed the same as the half-sized "minions" of the camp. Despite all that was in front of him, Johann still held the sword in his hand. He gripped it tighter as he assessed the situation. Faeyn stood next to him.

"So you have come out of your hole, Krath?" Faeyn scolded the giant. "Have you become so foolish as to risk the wrath of my father, the king? An arch mage? You know he will come after me and destroy you." Johann did not think antagonizing the giant was the best strategy, but kept silent.

King Krath the Warlock, as foul and fearsome as he was, was not the darkest or foulest creature in the VenKeth. Not compared to Morlith the Night Hag that haunted the swamps to the south or Gorefang the Old, a green dragon that claimed the forest in the north, or Lord Nusair, a death knight whose faltering castle stood far to the east, as well as others mentioned in other tales. However, he ruled a sizable chunk of VenKeth in the southwest and travelers feared him along the Forest Road. Those others left him alone. He had secured a pact with some spirit that gave him powers beyond those of other goblins. This, along with his cunning, allowed him to carve out a small kingdom.

"I expect that," Krath responded as he studied them both,

"but that will take some time, will it not? Does he even know you are gone yet? You both will be slaves deep in my mines by the time he knows about it, most likely. And he will never find you there. Be quiet and be prepared to move." He paused and called out before she could respond. "Forn! Bring me Forn! Now!" His eyes never left the two of them. "Search the boy and take his weapons! And how did he get a goblin blade?"

Johann brandished the sword in reaction, but the goblins only laughed. One of the oversized guards took his sword and groped him for other weapons. He found the elfin dagger in his belt in front, but missed the smaller throwing dagger originally given him by Baralas tucked under the tunic in the back. Now the goblins, all in a flurry, shoved the prisoners back into the camp between the boulders. Dawn arrived, though no sun revealed itself.

Krath sat down on a rock near the center of camp, pointing for the two prisoners to sit next to him on the ground as all the goblins surrounded them. They noticed what appeared to be the slave shuffle up on the other side of Krath. A human in a torn and dirty woolen tunic that must have been white at one time. His woolen pants looked the same. Rags bundled around his feet instead of shoes. The man looked recently beaten, with multiple bruises and black eyes, as well as fresh scars on his arms and calves. A heavy pack weighed on his back, causing him to hunch. Johann realized his broken spirit bent his back more than the pack. Both Faeyn and Johann recognized him after a moment. It was Jesper, Johann's tormentor from the caravan. Jesper never acknowledged either of them. Whether out of fear or brokenness, Johann never knew. How he came to be here is a tale for another time.

Krath called for the goblin, Forn, to come before him. Forn led the group that attacked the inn, the two soon discovered. He was a minor goblin leader known as a "whip." Whips grew slightly taller than the average goblin, similar in size to Johann, but not as massive as the boars. Johann guessed the boars were some type of elite guard for Krath. Forn came cowering before the king, fearing what may come next.

Krath let him grovel for a while before speaking. "Sloppy, you lazy bag of bones, letting them escape." Forn whimpered even more. "But I will consider that you got the princess here. So, I will not strip you of your wrinkled hide. We don't have time now, so they'll whip you when we get back. If you survive that, be thankful. Now get what's left of your crew ready to move." As Forn turned to scramble away, Krath smacked him with the blunt end of his spear. Forn tumbled to the ground and lay moaning for several minutes before crawling away.

Krath ignored him after that and without warning reached out and grabbed Faeyn's hand, yanking her to her feet. Taking his knife from his belt, he sliced her right palm. He turned the hand over to let the blood drip on the ground.

"Sit boy. I am not hurting her."

Krath let go of her. Now standing, Johann helped her wrap the injured hand in a torn cloth as Krath stirred his long, thick fingernail in the blood and dirt, muttering to himself.

He grunted, then growled to Johann, "Hand, boy." Johann looked him in the eye and presented his left hand. "Hmm, trying to act brave. Impress the girl, huh? I don't need you, may cut your throat instead. What will she think of that? Maybe nothing. Elfin don't tolerate mixed blood, you know."

But he only gave a shallow slash on the presented hand, showing his skill with the blade. He squeezed the hand, dripping the blood next to Faeyn's and began stirring it as before, releasing Johann. The others stood in ranks, ready to move out. Krath started studying the blood closer this time, however. He dug into his pouch and pulled out some knuckle dice with strange symbols on them, dropping the stained set in the blood while examining them. He scooped them up and dropped them again in a dented silver pan he had pulled out.

"Who are you, boy?" Giving an intense stare at Johann.

"He is just a farmer, helping at the inn. Let him go! He can't hurt you," Faeyn interjected.

"His blood says different. He is not at the inn now, is he? He's here somehow, with a goblin's sword in his hand, no less. But I didn't ask you! Name, boy!"

"Johann, son of Wain."

Krath stared at him and looked once more at the blood. "Tie their hands. Move out, you cowering rats! These two are in the middle with me. Back to the Keep!" Johann and Faeyn did not know what he saw in the blood, but it had scared the Warlock, even if he did not admit it. Johann certainly did not feel he could harm the great goblin, even with a sword.

CHAPTER 13
WHIPS AND CURSES

The goblins moved out, walking in undisciplined bunches of vague parallel lines, blundering through the brush. Johann and Faeyn walked in the midst of them with their hands tied in the front, stumbling occasionally over roots or other hidden hazards. The landscape shifted from flat to rolling hills as they moved in a southeasterly direction. It was fully day now, but no direct sunlight reached underneath the thick canopy. Krath kept the two youths near, walking just a few paces behind them. Jesper walked close next to him, following like a disciplined puppy.

Johann chanced a whisper to the maid when Krath turned to curse some minions. "I never got to ask, are you okay... I mean, hurt or anything?" He then added, "umm, your highness."

"Stop that! Just call me Faeyn. We're friends! Yes, I am fine, thank you. I'm very sorry you are captive, too. I didn't mean... I mean, thanks for coming to rescue me."

"Keep your mouths shut, you pale little pups! Unless you want a whip!" Krath barked.

"You're welcome, Princess," Johann whispered, feeling quite pleased with her comment. Just then, a small bullwhip cracked right by his head.

"Shut it or the next one will take off your ear!" snapped a goblin whip that was now marching right behind them. He snapped it above Johann's head again for fun.

With the cracking of the whip, the goblins all started jogging in fear, forcing the prisoners to do so as well. They trotted for another mile or two, getting deeper and deeper into the forest. The troop had spread out some as they moved and overall seemed more relaxed, now being in familiar territory. The trails became visibly worn and broader as they moved deeper into Krath's domain. Even the princess did not know how far it was to Goblins' Keep, hours or even days, perhaps. She knew Krath maintained outposts and camps throughout his kingdom and a few closer to the Forest Road. She suspected they would reach one of those first.

It took all of their energy to keep running, and the whip cracked over their head once in a while, making it hard for Johann to think. How were they going to get out of this? Were they going to be goblin slaves for the rest of their brief lives? The picture of Jesper would not leave his mind. It must not have taken long for him to break, judging by the time that they had last seen the caravan. It had just been a few weeks. How long will he last? Would Faeyn's father pay a ransom to get her out? Or maybe attack the goblins? The elfin king would probably do anything to get her back, but what about him? There was no one to pay for him. His parents did not even know where he was.

"Johann!" a voice popped into his head. It was Silvian! "Be ready! When you hear a noise, look for me on your left. Get the princess on my back as quickly as you can!"

"Okay. When?"

"Be ready!" He saw Faeyn perk up and assumed Silvian prepared her as well. He noticed Faeyn whispering and moving her hands. Straightway, there was a loud roar about thirty feet to their right. The minions and whips shrieked in fear as they ducked into the bushes. Johann jumped as well. At that moment, Silvian came, his silvery coat appearing to almost glow as he glided like an angelic being through the dark green of the forest. Goblins cowered or fled before his countenance and flashing hooves. As he reached the pair, his voice screamed out, promising doom to all that hated the light.

"Quickly! To me!" Silvian projected in their minds as he came running up. Faeyn ran to him and grabbed his mane as best she could with tied hands. Johann was right behind her, pushing her up. Without warning, someone grabbed him from behind and threw Johann to the ground. A goblin boar towered over him, sword in hand, reaching for the princess next. Johann fumbled for his dagger as Silvian gave the boar a rear kick. The guard crumbled several feet away.

Johann assumed Silvian would be off with the princess. It was too risky to delay. "Go!" he yelled as he tried to sit up. He then noticed the goblin with the whip cowering next to him. Dagger now in hand, he rolled and slashed at the creature, who shrieked and scrambled away. A sword lay on the ground where he left it. He shoved the dagger back into his belt and grabbed for the sword, standing up to cover Silvian's retreat.

Krath never cowered, but the roar fooled him, drawing him away from his prisoners. Once he realized the ruse, the appearance of the unicorn and the groveling of his minions enraged him. He turned back towards his prisoners to watch the large boar fly back from Silvian's kick. Cursing, he stretched out his hand, uttering strange sounds. A beam of energy burst from his upraised palm and streaked towards the princess. Johann now stood in between the beam and the unicorn. He had no time to react and to move would expose his allies to the beam. He braced himself for whatever pain was coming. Just as the beam reached him, they disappeared, blasting a smoking hole into a tree behind where they had stood.

CHAPTER 14
FLIGHT THROUGH THE FOREST

"Did you really think we would leave you behind?" asked the princess, letting go of her firm grip on his collar, for she had grabbed it at the last second. "That is what Silvian just told me."

"What happened? Where did that roar come from? I should be dead. That beam of light..." Johann's voice trailed off.

"Unicorns have the ability to teleport." Silvian interjected. "I would have preferred you on my back, but I can do it if you are close enough. You did not have to grab him, your highness. That was very thoughtful of you. I need a moment to rest, but we must move. We are less than a mile away from them and still deep within Krath's domain. Without my full horn, teleporting takes more out of me. And longer to recover."

"Yes, of course. I need a minute, too," Faeyn said. "They took me right from my bed." Johann cut the cords around her wrists, then she did the same for him. "The roar was an illusionist's trick. I did that. I know some magic." She ran her fingers through her glazed honey hair with a sigh, removing what sticks and leaves she could. She then braided it and tied it off. Next, she looked at her tattered, ankle length night-gown. She tore each side up to just above her knee for better mobility. Johann took some time to adjust his sword and dagger in his belt for riding as she prepped herself. He wished he had his bow, too. Once satisfied, she walked over and gave Johann a kiss on the cheek, to his shock and pleasure.

"That is for coming to find me." She did the same for Silvian.

"Time to go," stated Silvian, sounding less exhausted. "Up on my back." Johann climbed up first and pulled the princess up behind him. She wrapped her arms around his waist. Never before had he experienced a young woman's arms around him, but he found it pleasurable. Then they were off, heading north. "Watch your heads and hold tight. I am nimble and fleet of foot, but the branches are thick and twisted. Fallen trees are everywhere." Johann and Faeyn squatted low on his back and gripped with hands and legs, as they had no reins or saddle.

Silvian dashed through the trees, cutting and ducking and leaping as needed. It was noisier than he wished, but he wanted speed more than stealth at this point. It may not take long for the goblins to find them—or other enemies. He focused on reaching the Forest Road, which cut the vast expanse in half, but it was still many miles north. From there, they could stay on the road hoping the elfin find them, or travel into the Fae Lands farther north. It could be dangerous in the Fae Lands, too, but it was his original home and out of Krath's reach. The Fae Lands also bordered the elfin king's realm, farther northwest. The two on his back held on well, but he also made sure they did not fall.

The three of them made their way up a hill, towards an area that looked to have thinner brush. As they reached a small clearing on top, Silvian abruptly reared up, kicking. Johann barely held on, but managed as Faeyn clung to him. Three large furry creatures leaped in surprise.

"Vargin!" Faeyn cried. While vargin look much like wolves (though wolves would disagree), vargin are larger than wolves and more villainous. Wolves are creatures of the wild, descended from the first canine with the other beings brought forth by the Creator. They hunt to survive and live in packs or families. Vargin are evil creatures that kill for pleasure, bred and twisted from canine ancestors by fiends.

"Well, well," smirked the pack leader, as realization came to him. "Dinner has come to us this time. Elfin and human whelps on a hornless unicorn. You never know what you will see in this forest." The vargin moved to surround the three as Johann drew his sword.

"Look at that, Strong Jaw, he has a little goblin poker," laughed a second in response, named Red Fang.

"I wonder where he got that? Stealing from the goblins? Krath would like to know, I bet," Strong Jaw replied.

Without warning, Silvian leaped over Strong Jaw in front of him, forcing the vargin to leap out of the way. The beast recovered to snap at the unicorn's neck. The other two leaped at Silvian's legs, but fiery darts shot from Faeyn's hands as she cried out, hitting both of the beasts. They howled in pain at the fire and scurried out of the way. Johann slashed at Strong Jaw as they passed by him. Johann missed, but it foiled his attack. The three escaped down the front slope unscathed. They did not get far before excited howls reverberated through the forest after them.

"That howling will alert Krath to our whereabouts," warned Silvian. "I don't know if Strong Jaw is one of Krath's servants or if they roam wild. Either way, Krath will follow soon. And any other creature within miles."

Silvian leaped and darted through the thick canopy like a

fleet-footed deer, even with the two on his back. Unicorns are creatures of the forest, but so are the vargin and they did not fall far behind. The third beast, Swift Foot by name, ran the fastest. He snapped at the heels of the three, trying to hamstring his sylvan prey. Silvian kept him at bay, but it allowed the other vargin to gain on them. Johann slid around Silvian's back, being an inexperienced rider without reins and saddle. Faeyn held onto him with her hands and their silvery steed with her legs, helping to keep him stable. Finally, as Johann heard the others closing in, he took a slash at Swift Foot when it came up beside him, but feared hitting Silvian or Faeyn. To his surprise, Johann felt the sword dig deep, causing a loud whelp and almost ripping the sword out of his hand. The beast tumbled and did not get up.

"Well done!" encouraged Silvian in his mind and Faeyn gave him a squeeze.

The other two vargin checked on their own before resuming the hunt, but they proceeded with more caution. Apparently, the trio was not the easy prey the vargin first perceived. The unicorn gained on them for just a moment, but it didn't last. Vengeance now filled the remaining beasts' minds. Not for the love of their companion, but just from wicked natures and prideful hearts.

Silvian huffed as he turned to climb a small hill. This surprised Johann, because going up the slope slowed them down, allowing the vargin to gain a bit, but he trusted his friend. The unicorn then looped around the top of the hill to circle back.

"Be ready," he stated. "I cannot outrun them forever. But, fear not, I will protect you." Johann prepared his sword once again, now stained with blood. With great determination, they charged down the hill. Ferociously, they fell upon the vargin, catching Red Fang, the second beast, fully within their onslaught. Red Fang whelped in fear and fled with blood pouring out. For though the vargin are fiercer than wolves, they are also more cowardly. Strong Jaw, however, was a force. Cunning in wit, strong of will, and cruel of heart. He hated all creation, especially the Fae. He turned towards his three adversaries, bent on their destruction, his prime enemy being that of the unicorn.

Silvian reared, throwing off his two riders as he leaped to meet his newly gained nemesis. His coat shone once again, a light in a dark place. The two raged in battle, tooth and claw, hoof and fang, will against will. Light against dark. The sounds of the battle reverberated across the forest, but all Johann and Faeyn could do was watch. Johann stood in awe of the might of the creatures, having no experience with which to compare it. Then Silvian leaped away and fled east, with Strong Jaw close behind.

"Flee! Enter the Fae Lands, if you must! I will find you!" The words flashed in their minds. Then the two combatants disappeared into the gloom. The sounds of the battle continued to echo back to them as Silvian's light faded.

CHAPTER 15
A ROAD LESS TRAVELED

T he sun was setting in the outside world, but it was already beyond twilight as the two stumbled in the direction they estimated was north and west. Johann kept hoping to hear Silvian in their minds, but all remained silent. Exhaustion took them after the long day, and they found a small clearing that seemed safe. They both collapsed. Enna had put food in Johann's pack, but Krath had taken everything, so they did without. With their mouths dry and with stomachs grumbling, they settled down for the night.

Faeyn curled up next to him to stay warm, so he draped his cloak over them both. He did his best to comfort her. Johann tried to stay awake to watch for goblins and any other foul creatures, but failed. He dreamed of a young woman he had never seen before. She was about his age, he guessed, wearing a green dress with hair all the way down her back. The hair was red with small green leaves in it, but they seemed like they belonged there. She peaked shyly from behind a tree. He noticed her gesturing for him to come closer. Johann looked around to be sure nothing else was nearby. He stood up to see her better, but she hid again behind the tree. After inching from under Faeyn without waking her, he walked over to where he saw the girl, but he could not find her. He heard a slight giggle. She was hiding behind another tree the same distance away.

"Who are you? What are you doing here in the forest?" he asked in hushed tones."Are you lost? It is dangerous here."

"Can you help me?" She asked as she hid behind the tree again. "What is your name?"

"I will try. My name is Johann. What is yours?"

"Wonderful, Johann," she said, but a giggled escaped. "Please help me." Johann moved towards her again, but she was not to be found. He thought this was a strange dream.

"Are you hurt? Or lost? Did you get separated from a caravan? Come closer, let me see you and we can talk. I won't hurt you." Johann crept forward again. Out of nowhere, she was now standing next to him. She had large brown eyes and a big, bright smile lit up her face. She curled her arms around his right arm as her long hair brushed against him.

"My, you are young. And handsome. I need your help. Come with me. Let me show you." She started leading him farther away from camp. Something felt wrong to Johann, but she seemed so innocent, and she was very attractive. Not as attractive as Faeyn, but still beautiful and exotic.

"Dryad! Stop! Johann! Do not listen to her!" Johann heard the voice, but it seemed distant. Was that Faeyn? He felt guilty, but continued to let the redhead lead him.

"Dryad! He is not for you! Stop, I said, or you will regret it!" Faeyn commanded again.

"Alright, your Highness," the dryad pouted, letting go of his arm, but still standing close. Johann came to realize that he was not dreaming, but was truly seeing the dryad next to him.

"Where did you find him?" she smiled at him again. "I do not get to see many men here."

"Johann, let go of her and move away if you don't want to be a slave forever."

"Just a little fun, princess. I did not know he was yours." The dryad then turned to Johann. "A forever you will never regret." Her face beamed. He looked first at the dryad, then at Faeyn, who appeared very annoyed. Johann untangled himself from the redhead and stepped away.

"He is not 'mine,'" she said. "We are just friends. Now, how close are we to the Forest Road? How do we get to my home from here, dryad?" She continued to scowl.

"Yes, your highness," she said subdued. "The road is not far, just over there. You should find your way home from there if you travel west. But it is many miles still to the elfin realm and the goblins roam about looking for you." She then added as she looked at Johann, "You could stay here with me. I will keep you hid."

"We're going now, Johann." The stable boy nodded and went after Faeyn, who had started the direction the dryad had pointed without looking back to see if he followed.

"Bye, Johann!" the dryad called to him, making him turn red. "It was fun to meet you!"

"She is not a real girl, you know," Faeyn finally said after several minutes of silence. "They just pretend to be human to lure foolish men into their lairs, where bad things happen."

"Thank you for protecting me. I thought it was a dream."

"Dreaming of redheads, are we?" she replied as she kept walking in front of him without turning around. He didn't reply. He was not sure why she seemed so mad.

Johann was thankful when they found the Old Forest Road after a short walk. They popped out on it without realizing that it was there until they stepped out of the trees. They both felt exposed and looked both directions for enemies, but it was empty as far as they could see, which was not too far. The road was just a pair of wheel tracks in the thin grass and dirt, just wide enough for a large wagon. The old, thick branches of the trees hung over the road, letting in no more light than the rest of the forest.

"I think we are near the Fae Lands," Faeyn said. "That dryad would not be too far from the Lands. It would be north of the road. My father's realm is next to that, but it is still pretty far. Several days, for sure."

"Surely, they will be looking for you by now," Johann stated, trying to be hopeful. "Maybe we will see them on the road."

"I hope so! Still, Krath will be looking, too. He will not give up so easily. Using the road may also be easier for Silvian to find us."

"Yes," agreed Johann, but he was not too hopeful for Silvian. The battle seemed fierce, and he feared the worst for the unicorn.

After a short disagreement—actually, you could say argument (but Faeyn wouldn't admit that) — they stayed on the road, but moved with stealth. They also decided that if they had trouble, they would run into the forest on the north side of the road, away from Krath's kingdom. Of course, being quiet was a little easier since they were both annoyed with the other for a while and neither wanted to talk. So they preceded west on the road, heading back towards the inn from what they could tell. The road looked abandoned, except for evidence of Captain Caelan's caravan a few weeks before. Caelan's caravan had made it this far, at least. The road wound around hills with twists and turns, making it difficult to see ahead. Of course, that also helped them from being exposed too much as well.

In the forest's stillness, they could hear something

happening on the road ahead, and it did not sound like elfin. Johann led the duo, but Faeyn heard it first with her sharp elfin ears and whispered for him to stop. They listened for several minutes, noticing the sounds of chopping wood. As they crept closer, they heard grumbling amongst the industrious labor. The road climbed a large hill before it skirted the side below a steep bank. It seemed to come from the hillside around the bend. Near the top of the slope, the youth could see goblins stacking long logs parallel to the road. Behind the logs, they piled rocks bigger than their own heads. It was obvious they were preparing some type of trap or ambush above the road. They bent a small tree, set pins, and rigged a trip wire. A goblin whip used his instrument of pain generously while a goblin bred vargin sat nearby on guard. The goblin guardians did not grow as large as the wild ones, like Strong Jaw. At one point, it looked like everything would come tumbling down, causing the boss to shriek and run, which made everyone else run, too. But it held, and they resumed working after the whip called everyone back to work.

Johann and Faeyn studied them from the brush for a while, deciding what to do next. Within minutes, another band of goblins marched up from the south. The two whips conferred for a few minutes before the new crew started digging and building barricades. Johann made mental notes to himself in case he had the opportunity to warn someone, like another caravan.

In silence, they went around the trap and the goblin crews without even the vargin noticing, but it soon became obvious that more goblins were patrolling the road. Fortunately, they avoided them all without being seen.

"Krath has many more goblins than my father realized," Faeyn whispered. It was time to get off the road, head north and try the Fae Lands. "The Fae Lands are full of many amazing magical creatures, even more than the rest of the forest. Dryads, fairies, fauns, Noldin, a unicorn or two, and even centaurs after the fall migration." Not all of them were nice to humans, or even to elfin or dwarfin, for that matter, so the Lands could be just as dangerous as the rest of the forest. Faeyn was confident that she could navigate the Lands and avoid trouble.

"What are Noldin?" Johann asked. "I've heard of other creatures, but I never heard of a Noldin."

Faeyn smiled. "The Noldin are like wolves, but purer, more like a unicorn. Like Silvian. Legends claim celestials created them to counter the vargin and other evil manipulations of nature."

They traveled for a while in what they believed was a northwesterly direction. Their stomachs rumbled and their throats scratched. They talked little and stumbled more. Faeyn hoped to find a stream and maybe some berries, but warned, "you always had to be leery of such things in the Venerable Woods." It was just past mid-day when they thought they heard music. Flutes, to be exact.

"Elfin?" Johann hoped, his voice cracking.

"Fauns, I would guess," frowned Faeyn. "Maybe they have food and drink. Be careful, their music can charm the unaware. They may try to trick you. Just for fun. Pleasure is all they live for. They can be so impolite."

"Are they dangerous?"

"Never to elfin. But they can be deceptive. I hear they're skilled with swords. Mostly, beware of their carefree lifestyle. They live for themselves only. You never know when you may suffer from the consequences of their actions."

Johann followed Faeyn as they slinked closer. They found themselves on the edge of moss covered ruins. Dark gray flag-stones split by grass and brush stretched across the forest floor to form an ancient courtyard surrounded by broken walls of worked stone. Remains of a serpent statue lay crumbled amongst the walls. The forest had engulfed whatever civilization that had once thrived here millennia ago.

Faeyn stopped on the edge of the clearing behind a low moss-covered wall to look, and Johann squatted down beside her. In the center of the clearing was a large fire. Around the fire danced seven fauns, their hooves making a rhythmic clacking on the stone. Another danced in place to the side, playing his flute. The half man, half goats laughed and sung as they danced, drinking wine out of goblets and popping pieces of fruit in their mouths as they swirled by a long table piled with food. It was the most festive scene Johann had ever seen. The sight of the food and drink made their dry mouths burn and their empty stomachs growl.

"Come join us!" one of them shouted as he came closer. "Come dance and sing! We see you behind the wall, little elfin! And you, young man!" He stomped his cloven hooves and chugged his wine as it slopped down his beard. "The more the merrier!" He added, wiping his mouth with the back of his hand.

Shrugging, they both got up and entered the clearing.

"My, my, what have we here?" The one speaking seemed to be the leader, or at least the most vocal and friendly. "Gentle-fauns, Gentle-fauns! Look here! Why it is Princess Faeyn! What an honor!" He bowed to them. The festivities stopped, and they all looked at their guests. "And who is this with you? A human boy! What an unusual sight! Is he your servant?" It always amazed Johann that everyone in the Forest knew Princess Faeyn, even if she didn't know them.

"No," Faeyn said, annoyed. "This is Johann."

"A bodyguard, then? Or..?" he said, looking at the goblin sword.

"No! A friend, that is all! He works at the inn."

"An elfin friend! What an honor for you, Johann! They have never given us such prestige!" He bowed again. "Well, come join us, friend! Dance, sing! We have lots of food and drink to share!" The music started again and so did the dancing. The two of them went right to the food and drink. They did not want to be impolite, but thirst overruled etiquette. Faeyn ate without fear, so Johann did not hesitate after watching her. The fauns let them eat without interruption until they appeared to be satisfied. Then, they grabbed their hands and made them dance. It was quite exhausting! At first, they were stiff and worn from their troubles the last few days, but the mood soon had them laughing and enjoying themselves, forgetting all their recent trials. Johann wore himself out long before any of the others did. He was from a quiet and humble culture and not used to such public displays. He had never had wine before, either. Thankfully, they gave him the watered down wineskins.

Finally, they all took a break to eat some more as twilight settled in. The flute player stared at Johann and said, "Here is a tune I think you may appreciate!" He played an enchanting song, carrying Johann far away to distant lands. He imagined himself a knight riding off to slay dragons, conquer enemies and save damsels. Then he remembered Faeyn's warning and his mind returned. The charm had failed. The flute music stopped as the fauns laughed. "He is too wise to be charmed. And strong-willed," The flute player laughed again, but sounded disappointed.

Faeyn smiled at him. "Yes, he grows wiser." It pleased Johann he passed the test.

"So, why are you wandering around in the Lands, young princess? What brings you so far from the inn, Johann?"

"Krath kidnapped me. We escaped." Faeyn told them. That stopped the laughing.

"King Krath! The Warlock Goblin! Oh, my!"

"Is he following you? Where is your father?"

"I am sure they are looking for us, both my father and Krath." Faeyn added. "We do not know where either of them are. Have you seen anyone or heard anything?"

"Not at all! But they would not be in the Lands," they said. "Come, let's talk of happier things! This news is too troubling. Forget your trials! Now is for celebration!" The fauns stoked the fire and began the reveries all over again as darkness fell. Johann and Faeyn let them celebrate late into the night as they settled in to sleep after eating a bit more. For though it was fun to dance and forget the harsh realities of life for the moment, the continuous partying grew more and more empty as time passed. At least for now, they felt safe.

CHAPTER 16
QUITE THE TROUBLE

The two woke up before dawn to find the fauns passed out from the wine. As the two prepared breakfast and tried to plan what to do next, the fauns slowly stirred. The cries of distance howls getting closer interrupted their thoughts. The fauns wept in dismay and stumbled off with great haste without even trying to assist their guests, leaving behind all in a scattered mess. They feared an encounter with Krath, nor did they want to face the elfin king. This had always been one of their favorite places to celebrate, but they did not come back to the place for many a year. Johann and Faeyn looked at the food and gathered what they could as the howls drew ever nearer.

"The vargin must be tracking our scent! We cannot outrun them!" Johann exclaimed. "We can fight, but there may be too many. Do you have any ideas?"

"The food and wine. Let us try to cover our scent with it. Maybe it will confuse them. I have seen such things with our hunting dogs." So they poured the wine over themselves and rubbed themselves with the spiciest foods. They scattered about what they could not take with them. They grabbed some drinking skins and a bag of food. Just then, a hawk landed on the ruined wall by Faeyn.

"Medwin! You found us! And you are all healed!" Faeyn exclaimed. The bird gave a screech in reply.

"Is help coming? Is it close by? Ask him!" Johann's nerves were on edge. The howls sounded closer.

"I cannot understand him without Silvian. I cannot use telepathy. But I think he can understand me. Medwin, tell my father where we are!" The hawk named Sharp-eye cried again and flew southwest a short distance. He cried again.

"Follow him!" Johann pointed. "Maybe they are nearby." They fled as the howls moved closer. The scattered food distracted the vargin in more ways than one, but it was not long before they were once again pursuing their prey.

The fleeing youth heard howls coming from both the left and right. The beasts maneuvered to cut off their escape. When the vargin came into sight behind, Johann took a stand. He found a place suitable to fight, fearing to be pounced on from behind like a deer. Faeyn stopped also and came to stand next to him. The beasts surrounded them within minutes, growling and threatening, some with goblins astride their backs like steeds. Johann recognized Red Fang standing a head higher than the others, his wounds treated by the goblins. No one moved as Johann twisted and turned to monitor all of them, even the ones behind. He doubted Krath wanted prisoners this time. The answer came soon enough when a goblin whip poked them with a spear, then pointed south. Once again, he gave up his sword. Medwin circled above them, gave a last encouraging cry, and raced away. Johann prayed the elfin searched nearby, but had little hope. Who knows what Krath would do once they stood before him?

Johann knew exactly where they were as they faced Krath

once again. The forest darkened in the presence of the goblin king and his army. He no longer lead just a few patrols, but hundreds of goblins hustled about entrenching themselves to prepare for battle. His cubit long knife casually rested in his hand as he used it to pick his teeth, streaks of dried blood darkening the blade. His heavy spear and iron banded shield leaned on a tree within reach. A pan sat next to him, bone knuckles scattered within among the dried blood. Fresh wounds marked his forearms. Jesper stood close by, holding his massive iron mace.

"You two are quite the trouble," Krath stated, "and I am about done with you both." He continued to pick his teeth. "I don't care about you, boy, your time is up. The princess, however, I may need yet. But I will give your father a corpse before I let him have you back whole again."

As he spoke, a cry went up from the goblin army. The elfin assault had begun. Arrows flew with deadly accuracy and fire balls erupted against goblin barricades. Bolts of lightning struck the front lines and the goblin archers behind. The air tingled with magic that even Johann could sense to his awe. Forces of will strove against one another. Minions fled past the warlock, but the goblin whips took up their tools to keep the troops in line. The great boars roared challenges and banged spear against shield. But the goblins fell back from the intense attack of the elfin. Krath seemed calm despite such an onslaught. Certainly, he knew his goblins could not withstand high elfin warriors in the open forest, even with his superior numbers and entrenched position. It dawned on Johann that the warlock was drawing the elfin into a trap.

Krath shoved the dagger at Jesper as he snatched the mace, his eyes never leaving Johann. He towered over Johann, brandishing his mace overhead for a crushing blow. The youth braced himself, searching for a defense as he pushed the princess away. But the blow never landed. Something struck the self-made king from behind, penetrating deep beneath his boiled leather armor. Krath arched his back, swinging his fisted hand in a circle, bellowing in rage. The blow caught Jesper in the head, knocking him to the ground, and yanking the bloody knife out of his back.

Faeyn shot magical darts from her right hand, hitting Krath's side, burning the tunic and boiled leather. Rage blocked out everything but vengeance. With mace in hand, he poured out his fury at the slave who had dared to stab him. Johann grabbed Faeyn's hand and fled, hoping Jesper's sacrifice would not be in vain.

Goblins scattered in all directions as elfin arrows struck their marks with great precision. In response, a wave of shield-bearing boars and ferocious vargin swooped down for a counterattack. Chaos ruled as the elfin advance halted. Johann knew they had to get through the goblins without getting killed by either side.

CHAPTER 17
LITTLE WARRIOR

"This way! Quickly!" Johann raced up the steep slope. "Where are you going? My father is the other way!"

They ran right into Red Fang. The beast had been watching them and waiting for an opportunity of vengeance. He blocked their path, stopping them in their tracks. Johann had no sword to defend himself this time. Red Fang charged them, both youths dodging snapping jaws. Red Fang pinned Johann, going for the throat as he knocked the princess away with his tail. The boy struggled to keep the bare teeth away with his forearm across the beast's neck, saliva and hot breath washing his face. He fumbled for his hidden dagger. As the vargin inched closer, Johann jammed the dagger into his neck. Blood spilled over him as the beast gurgled and collapsed. Johann gripped his weapon and rolled the body off him. After a shudder of fear ran through him, the two continued their scramble up the slope.

"Run, princess! Run, little warrior! But there is no place to run! You may never see the mines, but you will never see your homes again! Men and elfin will come here to lament your graves! If any of them survive." The warlock loped up the slope behind them. Krath had not forgotten them despite his rage. His anger intensified, and he determined to destroy them, even if all else failed. He taunted and cursed them as he drew near. Johann feared he may be right. The stable boy gripped the blood covered throwing dagger that Baralas had given him.

Krath laughed. "Little warrior with his toothpick thinks he can fight me? Ha, I will crush your head, then hers." Krath had stopped running but now sauntered up with his mace, an eye on each of the two. But Johann wasn't even looking at Krath. Instead, he studied the slope above him. Goblins continued to fall back as the resistance eased and even the great boars failed. Elfin pushed forward, closer to Krath's trap.

With as much concentration as he could muster, trembling with fear, knowing he had only one shot, he threw the dagger as Baralas had taught him. He felt the miniscule difference in weight with fresh blood on the blade as it slipped away. Krath and Faeyn both watched the dagger spin off his hand as time slowed. The blade rotated, tiny drops of blood spraying as it crossed the distance. But he did not throw it at Krath or any other goblin. With a hardy thud, the dagger stuck into a log. But the blade first sliced across the trip wire of the trap, just like back at the inn, where Baralas cut ribbons or snuffed candles with his knives in the shows. One strand after another twisted away as the rope stretched under the tension until finally giving way with a snap. With a tremendous rumble, logs and rocks tumbled down, destroying all in its path.

In that moment, Krath understood what he had seen in the boy's blood as the dust cloud engulfed them all. This simple farm boy, with the toss of a dagger, had not only taken his life, but had also crumbled his entire kingdom. The avalanche, planned for the elfin, instead crushed the fleeing army of the warlock. As Krath came to his end, a pain filled screech escaped above the rubble. The wicked spirit who had given the warlock his special powers rose from the debris and separated itself from the broken body. It hovered for a moment, then fled, in search of a new host to enslave without a second thought about the goblin king.

"Faeyn! Faeyn! Are you okay?" Johann called for her through the dust.

"Johann! Johann! Yes, I am safe! Are you hurt?"

"No. I am fine." They held each other for a moment in relief as the dust cloud thinned around them. Silvian found them that way when he came running up.

"Your father will be pleased to see you both, as am I!" Silvian rejoiced.

"Silvian! You are alive! We were so afraid for you!" Faeyn hugged him.

"Yes, Strong Jaw was fierce, but I overcame him in the end. I have a few fresh scars, however. I am getting old for such battles anymore. But not too old! I am glad you kept you wits about you and overcame the goblin king. I searched for you after defeating the vargin, but found the elfin instead. Now hop up and I will take you to see your father. He is looking for you!"

Johann pulled himself up before helping her get behind him. Then, quick as a wink, they were off to see the good king of the forest.

CHAPTER 18

A HERO NOW

The elfin dressed Johann in a sky blue silk top with silver trim, fine woolen trousers, and high leather boots. A pin with the royal stag seal was on his chest. A cloak of deeper blue hung on his left shoulder. It was the finest clothes he ever seen, much less worn. Tailor-made for the special banquet in honor of their victory and the rescue of the princess. The beauty of the elfin realm they named Haeren-Vale stunned him. He was still within the boundaries of the forest, but it was not so gloomy here. Light streamed through the white trees with twisted trunks and deep green leaves. Blossoms were everywhere, inside and out, even though it was after Mid-Summer's Day. Great vineyards and orchards were in abundance throughout the realm. Grape vines climbed the cherry wood lattice at the entrance to each hall of white stone. Johann felt so privileged to be here. And out of place.

Next to him dined the princess, her hair now combed and elegantly styled. A web of pearls draped her head, a thin silver tiara decorated her brow. He always thought she looked beautiful in her simple maid dress, but she was absolutely stunning now in her green silk gown. She looked to be everything a regal daughter should be. She was supposed to be sitting with her parents and siblings, but she insisted on being seated with him. The innkeepers, Erdan and Enna, sat with them, too. Among those also at the feast were men, rangers of the hidden abbey, who came to the aid of the elfin. Earlier, the king introduced Johann to Devarim, Ranger Lord and Sage, Chief of the Council, Wise Protector of the Abbey. The young ranger who had killed the four goblins at Threshold Pass was also there. He told Johann that he knew nothing about the princess. He just knew they were up to mischief. Of course, Silvian, Medwin, and Baralas were there, too.

When the moment arrived, Faeyn took Johann's hand and walked him to the front of the hall where the Elfin Lord Faeranduil, her father, awaited them. Silvian stood on one side and Baralas stood on the other side of the king, fully healed of his wounds.

"First, let us take a moment of silence to remember the man and slave Jesper, who gave his life so that my daughter may live. To sacrifice your own life for another is worthy of the greatest honor. It is a noble act that even a helpless slave can do for another. May we all promise, in honor of him, we will do all we can to find and free others slaves that may still be in the forest."

After the moment of silence, the king continued.

"Now, in honor of you protecting my youngest daughter, Princess Faeyn Secula, at a potential cost of your own life, and for overcoming the enemy of our people, the goblin king Krath the Warlock, we hereby name you Hir Johann d'Caun, royal guard of HaerenVale and personal honor guard to Princess Faeyn. This shall stand for the rest of your days." The king waited until the clapping ended. "Also, we give you these gifts to go with your new title: first the dagger that was retrieved from the forest, that was originally given to you by Hir Baralas, and with which you slew the goblin king." A servant came, took the dagger and its new sheath, and tucked it behind his belt. "We also give you this sword, crafted by the royal smiths, with which you may better protect the princess, rather than using a crude goblin blade." The king winked at him and smiled as the servant took it and tied it to his waist. "Finally, we give you this hand crafted hunting bow and a quiver of arrows because you lost your own while rescuing the princess." The servant presented them to Johann, who took them with a bow. "You are always welcome in our realm of HaerenVale, though you must always guard its secrets. Remember, you may be called upon to fulfill your duties as guardian of the realm at any time. Hir Baralas will see to it."

Baralas spoke next. "Just so you fully understand how great an honor the king bestowed upon you, this title granted to you is equivalent to you being knighted in your own realm. But this is even rarer for a human to receive it among the high elfin. You have a brave and noble heart, young Hir Johann d'Caun. That makes you a prince among men, no matter how others regard your social status. Remember that always." The words astounded Johann, for this was the first time Baralas had not called him "boy."

Johann bowed low, humbled by all the honor he received for his deeds. Such attention was beyond him. Everyone at the banquet cheered and honored him before he could sit down again.

"What will I say to my family? What will they think of these gifts? Can I tell them? I am due to fetch the milk for the inn the day after tomorrow! They do not even know I was gone from the inn! I can't imagine all this has happened in less than a week! It changed my life forever."

"You may tell them," the princess responded. "and please

tell them hello. I do not know when I will ever see them again. Johann, I am not going back to the inn. My father wants me here. But you must go back."

"Yes, we still need your help," Erdan said. Enna nodded. "Morgrim will not be back for weeks yet."

The truth slowly dawned on him. "You are not coming back? I... I will miss you. Faeyn, I..I...." He could not finish.

She smiled, "I know. Johann, I love you, too. But it is not for elfin and men to be in love or to marry. The creator has separated our races. But do not worry, I will see you again." She kissed his cheek and squeezed his hand.

The affirmation of love tore Johann's heart, for he could never be with her. It would be lonely at the inn.

"Cheer up, Johann, I heard Lord Devarim asking about you," Enna stated. "He may offer you training at the abbey. Or perhaps your king will train you as a knight when he hears!" The thought of his king hearing about him, a simple farm boy, and offering him training as a knight, seemed unbelievable. But he was "simple" no longer.

"And you can work at the inn as long as you like!" Erdan added. "You are a hero now. Others will come just to meet you!"

***

A few days later, Johann was guiding the wagon along the grassy two-track on his way home to get the milk and other produce for the inn. Silvian seemed to have a chipper step since they had returned to the inn. As noble a creature as he was, serving others delighted him. I guess that is one reason he was so noble. He told the elfin king he would like to stay at the inn for a while and be with Johann. They had become such great friends. The king and the princess both approved. Johann was glad to have such a friend and so was Silvian.

The vast forest was behind him, but he was a part of it now, too. He was back in his simple work clothes, but he was not the same person. The summer at the inn had promised to be exciting, but it had passed all his expectations. He did not yet know all the ways it had changed him, how he had grown. (However, his mother noticed right away.) He was not poor any longer, for the king had also given him a small purse full of gold and silver. Maybe he would go to the ranger's abbey, or go back to HaerenVale to train with Baralas. Perhaps he would train as a knight. Who knows what the future would hold? For now, he needed to fulfill his original agreement to be the stable boy for the summer. It was the right thing to do.

As soon as the inn was out of sight, a large white stag leaped onto the road in front of them as it had once before. Its sapphire blue eyes gazed upon the two. Silvian halted and called out. Then the unicorn bowed to the creature, for here was someone more righteous than even him. Johann understood now that all that happened was not by chance, but providential. There was a purpose to it all. Time disappeared, and he knew not how long they stayed. Then the broad antlered stag continued on its way, soon lost in the chin-high grasses. Silvian and Johann continued on to his home, with songs in their hearts.

The End

RANGER'S CALLING

A new epic fantasy novel series set in the same world of Veardalan

Released March 2025

Rangers Calling: The Fires of Wynchell

A far greater calling than He imagined. One that will test all his skills and wisdom.

Young Galieb trained among the elite Qoholet, a hidden society of highly skilled and learned rangers sages. But even among this tight knit community, he feels like an outsider, known as the "Half-elfin." Ready to find adventure and discover his destiny, the ranger travels north, following rumors of brutal raiders known as eshkin. But as Galieb fights eshkin, he believes there may be something else behind the dead sheep and missing villagers. Will he break under the fiery trials or emerge reforged?

An epic fantasy adventure with rangers, knights, wizards, and other heroes. If you like Dungeons and Dragons, J R R Tolkien, mythical creatures, good versus evil, and heroic deeds, you will enjoy this fantasy novel.

No romance or romance is secondary to story. Written for young men of all ages. Classified as Noblebright or Nobledark. Christian themes and theological questions.

Purchase Here:

First book in series.

Want more from Raymond Keith?

Sign up for my newsletter to get the latest updates and a free short story.

Find maps and more about the world of Veardalan on my website here:

ABOUT THE AUTHOR

Raymond grew up wandering the woods and fields of Pennsylvania looking for elves, goblins and dragons. He is fascinated with all of God's creation, both the natural and supernatural, talking to every animal he meets. To rest from reality, he would create stories for himself, but now shares them with others. As a servant of the True King, Christ, Raymond is currently assigned as a state park manager in southeast Montana. He lives with his enchanting bride and has been given an amazing daughter.